# LET ME HEAR YOU WHISPER

## a play by PAUL ZINDEL

## Drawings by Stephen Gammell

Harper & Row, Publishers

New York, Evanston, San Francisco, London

*to Matilda Rowan*
*my wonderful aunt*

# CHARACTERS

**Helen:** A little old cleaning lady who lives alone in a one-room apartment and spends most of her spare time feeding stray cats and dogs. She has just been hired to scrub floors in a laboratory that performs rather strange experiments with dolphins.

**Miss Moray:** A briskly efficient custodial supervisor who has to break Helen in to her new duties at the laboratory. She has a face that is so uptight she looks like she either throws stones at pigeons or teaches Latin.

**Dr. Crocus:** The dedicated man of science who devises and presides over the weird experiments.

**Mr. Fridge:** Assistant to Dr. Crocus. He is so loyal and uncreative that if Dr. Crocus told him to stick his head in the mouth of a shark, he'd do it.

**Dan:** A talky janitor, also under Miss Moray's control, who at every chance ducks out of the Manhattan laboratory for a beer at the corner bar.

**A Dolphin:** The subject of an experiment being performed by Dr. Crocus.

**Setting:** *The action takes place in the hallway, laboratory and specimen room of a biology experimentation association located in Manhattan near the Hudson River.*

**Time:** *The action begins with the night shift on a Monday and ends the following Friday.*

# ACT I / Scene 1

(DR. CROCUS *and* MR. FRIDGE *are leaving the laboratory where they have completed their latest experimental tinkering with a dolphin, and they head down a corridor to the elevator. The elevator door opens and* MISS MORAY *emerges with* HELEN.)

MISS MORAY: Dr. Crocus. Mr. Fridge. I'm so glad we've run into you. I want you to meet Helen.

HELEN: Hello.
(DR. CROCUS *and* MR. FRIDGE *nod and get on elevator.*)

MISS MORAY: Helen is the newest member of our Custodial Engineering Team.

(MISS MORAY *and* HELEN *start down the hall.*)

MISS MORAY: Dr. Crocus is the guiding heart here at the American Biological Association Development for the Advancement of Brain Analysis. For short, we call it "Abadaba."

HELEN: I guess you have to.
(*They stop at a metal locker at the end of the hall.*)

MISS MORAY: This will be your locker and your key. Your equipment is in this closet.

HELEN: I have to bring in my own hangers, I suppose.

MISS MORAY: Didn't you find Personnel pleasant?

HELEN: They asked a lot of crazy questions.

MISS MORAY: Oh, I'm sorry. (*pause*) For instance.

HELEN: They wanted to know what went on in my head when I'm watching television in my living room and the audience laughs. They asked if I ever thought the audience was laughing at *me*.

MISS MORAY (*laughing*): My, oh, my! (*pause*) What did you tell them?

HELEN: I don't have a TV.

MISS MORAY: I'm sorry.

HELEN: I'm not.

MISS MORAY: Yes. Now, it's really quite simple. That's our special soap solution. One tablespoon to a gallon of hot water, if I may suggest.
(HELEN *is busy running water into a pail which fits into a metal stand on wheels.*)

MISS MORAY: I'll start you in the laboratory. We like it done first. The specimen room next, and finally the hallway. By that time we'll be well toward morning, and if there are a few minutes left, you can polish the brass strip. (*She points to brass strip which runs around the corridor, halfway between ceiling and floor.*) Ready? Fine. (*They start down the hall,* MISS MORAY *thumbing through papers on a clipboard.*)

MISS MORAY: You were with one concern for fourteen years, weren't you? Fourteen years with the

3

Metal Climax Building. That's next to the Radio City Music Hall, isn't it, dear?

HELEN: Uh-huh.

MISS MORAY: They sent a marvelous letter of recommendation. My! Fourteen years on the seventeenth floor. You must be very proud. Why did you leave?

HELEN: They put in a rug.
(MISS MORAY *leads* HELEN *into the laboratory, where* DAN *is picking up.*)

MISS MORAY: Dan, Helen will be taking Marguerita's place. Dan is the night porter for the fifth through ninth floors.

DAN: Hiya!

HELEN: Hello. (*She looks around.*)

MISS MORAY: There's a crock on nine you missed, and the technicians on that floor have complained about the odor.
(HELEN *notices what appears to be a large tank of water with a curtain concealing its contents.*)

HELEN: What's that?

MISS MORAY: What? Oh, that's a dolphin, dear. But don't worry about anything except the floor. Dr. Crocus prefers us not to touch either the equipment or the animals.

HELEN: Do you keep him cramped up in that all the time?

MISS MORAY: We have a natatorium for it to exercise in, at Dr. Crocus's discretion.

HELEN: He really looks cramped.
(MISS MORAY *closes a curtain which hides the tank.*)

MISS MORAY: Well, you must be anxious to begin. I'll make myself available at the reception desk in the hall for a few nights in case any questions arise. Coffee break at two and six A.M. Lunch at four A.M. All clear?

HELEN: I don't need a coffee break.

MISS MORAY: Helen, we all need Perk-You-Ups. All of us.

6

HELEN: I don't want one.

MISS MORAY: They're compulsory. (*pause*) Oh, Helen, I know you're going to fit right in with our little family. You're such a *nice* person. (*She exits.*)
(HELEN *immediately gets to work, moving her equipment into place and getting down on her hands and knees to scrub the floor.* DAN *exits.* HELEN *gets in a few more rubs, glances at the silhouette of the dolphin's tank behind the curtain, and then continues. After a pause, a record begins to play.*)

RECORD: "Let me call you sweetheart,
         I'm in love with you.
         Let me hear you whisper
         That you love me, too."

(HELEN'S *curiosity makes her open the curtain and look at the dolphin. He looks right back at her. She returns to her work, singing "Let Me Call You Sweetheart" to herself, missing a word here and there; but her eyes return to the dolphin. She becomes uncomfortable under his stare and tries to ease her discomfort by playing peek-a-boo with him. There is no response and*

7

*she resumes scrubbing and humming. The dolphin then lets out a bubble or two and moves in the tank to bring his blowhole to the surface.*)

DOLPHIN: Youuuuuuuuuuuu.
(HELEN *hears the sound, assumes she is mistaken, and goes on with her work.*)

DOLPHIN: Youuuuuuuuuuuu.
(HELEN *has heard the sound more clearly this time. She is puzzled, contemplates a moment, and then decides to get up off the floor. She closes the curtain on the dolphin's tank and leaves the laboratory. She walks the length of the hall to* MISS MORAY, *who is sitting at a reception desk near the elevator.*)

MISS MORAY: What is it, Helen?

HELEN: The fish is making some kinda funny noise.

MISS MORAY: Mammal, Helen. It's a mammal.

HELEN: The mammal's making some kinda funny noise.

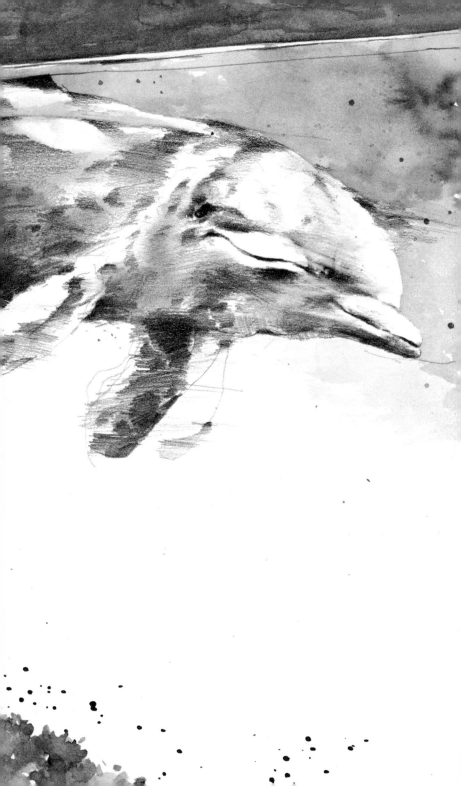

MISS MORAY: Mammals are supposed to make funny noises.

HELEN: Yes, Miss Moray.
(HELEN *goes back to the lab. She continues scrubbing.*)

DOLPHIN: Youuuuuuuuuuuu.
(*She apprehensively approaches the curtain and opens it. Just then* DAN *barges in. He goes to get his reaching pole, and* HELEN *hurriedly returns to scrubbing the floor.*)

DAN: Bulb out on seven.

HELEN: What do they have that thing for?

DAN: What thing?

HELEN: That.

DAN: Yeah, he's something, ain't he? (*pause*) They're tryin' to get it to talk.

HELEN: Talk?

DAN: Uh-huh, but he don't say nothing. They

had one last year that used to laugh. It'd go "heh heh heh heh heh heh heh." Then they got another one that used to say, "Yeah, it's four o'clock." Everybody took pictures of that one. All the magazines and newspapers.

HELEN: It just kept saying "Yeah, it's four o'clock"?

DAN: Until it died of pneumonia. They talk outta their blowholes, when they can talk, that is. Did you see the blowhole?

HELEN: No.

DAN: Come on and take a look.

HELEN: I don't want to look at any blowhole.

DAN: Miss Moray's at the desk. She won't see anything.
(HELEN *and* DAN *go to the tank. Their backs are to the lab door and they don't see* MISS MORAY *open the door and watch them.*)

DAN: This one don't say anything at all. They been playing that record every seven minutes for months, and it can't even learn a single word. Don't even say "Polly want a cracker."

MISS MORAY: Helen?
(HELEN *and* DAN *turn around.*)

MISS MORAY: Helen, would you mind stepping outside a moment?

HELEN: Yes, Miss Moray.

DAN: I was just showing her something.

MISS MORAY: Hadn't we better get on with our duties?

DAN: All right, Miss Moray.
(MISS MORAY *guides* HELEN *out into the hall, and puts her arm around her as though taking her into her confidence.*)

MISS MORAY: Helen, I called you out here because . . . well, frankly, I need your help.

HELEN: He was just showing me . . .

MISS MORAY: Dan is an idle-chatter breeder. How

many times we've told him, "Dan, this is a scientific atmosphere you're employed in and we would appreciate a minimum of subjective communication." So—if you can help, Helen—and I'm sure you can, enormously—we'd be so grateful.

HELEN: Yes, Miss Moray.
(MISS MORAY *leads* HELEN *back to the lab.*)

MISS MORAY: Now, we'll just move directly into the specimen room. The working conditions will be ideal for you in here.
(HELEN *looks ready to gag as she looks around the specimen room. It is packed with specimen jars of all sizes. Various animals and parts of animals are visible in their formaldehyde baths.*)

MISS MORAY: Now, you will be responsible not only for the floor area but the jars as well. A feather duster—here—is marvelous.
(MISS MORAY *smiles and exits. The sound of music and voice from beyond the walls floats over.*)

RECORD: "Let me call you sweetheart . . ."
(HELEN *gasps as her eyes fall upon one particular jar in which is floating a preserved human brain. The lights go down, ending Act I, Scene 1.*)

## ACT I / Scene 2

(*It is the next evening.* HELEN *pushes her equipment into the lab. She opens the curtain so she can watch the dolphin as she works. She and the dolphin stare at each other.*)

HELEN: Youuuuuuuuuuuu. (*She pauses, watches for a response.*) Youuuuuuuuuuuu. (*Still no response. She turns her attention to her scrubbing for a moment.*) Polly want a cracker? Polly want a cracker? (*She wrings out a rag and resumes work.*) Yeah, it's four o'clock. Yeah, it's four o'clock. Polly want a cracker at four o'clock? (*She laughs at her own joke, then goes to the dolphin's tank and notices how sad he looks. She reaches her hand in and just touches the top of his head. He squirms and likes it.*)

HELEN: Heh heh heh heh heh heh heh heh heh. (MISS MORAY *gets off the elevator and hears the peculiar sounds coming from the laboratory. She puts her ear against the door.*)

HELEN: Heh heh heh heh heh . . .

MISS MORAY (*entering*): Look how nicely the floor's coming along! You must have a special rinsing technique.

HELEN: Just a little vinegar in the rinse water.

MISS MORAY: You brought the vinegar yourself, just so the floors . . . they are sparkling, Helen. Sparkling! (*She pauses—looks at the dolphin, then at* HELEN.) It's marvelous, Helen, how well you've adjusted.

HELEN: Thank you, Miss Moray.

MISS MORAY: Helen, the animals here are used for experimentation, and. . . . Well, take Marguerita. She had fallen in love with the mice. All three hundred of them. She seemed shocked when she found out Dr. Crocus was...using... them at the rate of twenty or so a day in connection with electrode implanting. She noticed them missing after a while and when I told her they'd been decapitated, she seemed terribly upset.

HELEN: What do they want with the fish—mammal?

MISS MORAY: Well, dolphins may have an intelligence equal to our own. And if we can teach them our language—or learn theirs—we'll be able to communicate.

HELEN: I can't understand you.

MISS MORAY (*louder*): Communicate! Wouldn't it be wonderful?

HELEN: Oh, yeah. . . . They chopped the heads off three hundred mice? That's horrible.

MISS MORAY: You're so sensitive, Helen. Every laboratory in the country is doing this type of work. It's quite accepted.

HELEN: Every laboratory cutting off mouse heads!

MISS MORAY: Virtually . . .

18

HELEN: How many laboratories are there?

MISS MORAY: I don't know. I suppose at least five thousand.

HELEN: Five thousand times three hundred . . . that's a lot of mouse heads. Can't you just have one lab chop off a couple and then spread the word?

MISS MORAY: Now, Helen—this is exactly what I mean. You will do best not to become fond of the subject animals. When you're here a little longer you'll learn . . . well . . . there are some things you just have to accept on faith.
(MISS MORAY *exits, leaving the lab door open for* HELEN *to move her equipment out.*)

DOLPHIN: Whisper . . . (HELEN *pauses a moment.*) Whisper to me. (*She exits as the lights go down, ending the scene.*)

## ACT I / Scene 3

(*It is the next evening.* HELEN *goes from her locker to the laboratory.*)

DOLPHIN: Hear...

HELEN: What?

DOLPHIN: Hear me...
(DAN *barges in with his hamper, almost frightening* HELEN *to death. He goes to dolphin's tank.*)

DAN: Hiya, fella! How are ya? That reminds me. Gotta get some formaldehyde jars set up by Friday. If you want anything just whistle.
(*He exits. Helen goes to the tank and reaches her hand out to pet the dolphin.*)

20

HELEN: Hear. (*pause*) Hear.

DOLPHIN: Hear.

HELEN: Hear me.

DOLPHIN: Hear me.

HELEN: That's a good boy.

DOLPHIN: Hear me...

HELEN: Oh, what a pretty fellow. Such a pretty fellow.
(MISS MORAY *enters.*)

MISS MORAY: What are you doing, Helen?

HELEN: I... uh...

MISS MORAY: Never mind. Go on with your work.
(MISS MORAY *surveys everything, then sits on a stool.* DAN *rushes in with large jars on a wheeled table.*)

DAN: Scuse me, but I figure I'll get the formaldehyde set up tonight.

MISS MORAY: Very good, Dan.

HELEN (*noticing the dolphin is stirring*): What's the formaldehyde for?

MISS MORAY: The experiment series on . . . the dolphin will . . . terminate on Friday. That's why it has concerned me that you've apparently grown . . . fond . . . of the mammal.

HELEN: They're gonna kill it?

DAN: Gonna sharpen the handsaws now. Won't have any trouble getting through the skull on this one, no, sir. (*He exits.*)

HELEN: What for? Because it didn't say anything? Is that what they're killing it for?

MISS MORAY: Helen, no matter how lovely our intentions, no matter how lonely we are and how much we want people or animals . . . to like us . . . we have no right to endanger the genius about us. Now, we've spoken about this before.
(HELEN *is dumbfounded as* MISS MORAY *exits.* HELEN *gathers her equipment and looks at the dolphin, which is staring desperately at her.*)

DOLPHIN: Help. (*pause*) Please help me.
(*HELEN is so moved by the cries of the dolphin she looks ready to burst into tears as the lights go down, ending Act I.*)

# ACT II

(*The hall: It is the night that the dolphin is to be dissected. Elevator doors open and* HELEN *gets off, nods, and starts down the hall.* MISS MORAY *comes to* HELEN *at closet.*)

MISS MORAY: I hope you're well this evening.

HELEN: When they gonna kill it?

MISS MORAY: Don't say kill, Helen. You make it sound like murder. Besides, you won't have to go into the laboratory at all this evening.

HELEN: How do they kill it?

MISS MORAY: Nicotine mustard, Helen. It's very humane. They inject it.

HELEN: Maybe he's a mute.

MISS MORAY: Do you have all your paraphernalia?

HELEN: Some human beings are mute, you know. Just because they can't talk we don't kill them.

MISS MORAY: It looks like you're ready to open a new box of steel wool.

HELEN: Maybe he can type with his nose. Did they try that?

MISS MORAY: Now, now, Helen—

HELEN: Miss Moray, I don't mind doing the lab.

MISS MORAY: Absolutely not! I'm placing it off limits for your own good. You're too emotionally involved.

HELEN: I can do the lab, honest. I'm not emotionally involved.

MISS MORAY (*motioning her to the specimen-room door*): Trust me, Helen. Trust me.

HELEN (*reluctantly disappearing through the door*): Yes, Miss Moray.

(MISS MORAY *stations herself at the desk near the elevator and begins reading her charts.* HELEN *slips out of the specimen room and into the laboratory without being seen. The lights in the lab are out and moonlight from the window casts eerie shadows.*)

DOLPHIN: Help.

(HELEN *opens the curtain. The dolphin and she look at each other.*)

DOLPHIN: Help me.

HELEN: You don't need me. Just say something to them. Anything. They just need to hear you say something. . . . You want me to tell 'em? I'll tell them. I'll just say I heard you say "Help." (*pauses, then speaks with feigned cheerfulness*) I'll go tell them.

DOLPHIN: Noooooooooooooooo.

(HELEN *stops. Moves back toward tank.*)

HELEN: They're gonna kill you!

DOLPHIN: Plaaaaan.

HELEN: What?

DOLPHIN: Plaaaaaaan.

HELEN: Plan? What plan?
(DAN *charges through the door and snaps on the light.*)

DAN: Uh-oh. Miss Moray said she don't want you in here.
(HELEN *goes to* DR. CROCUS's *desk and begins to look at various books on it.*)

HELEN: Do you know anything about a plan?

DAN: She's gonna be mad. What plan?

HELEN: Something to do with . . . (*She indicates the dolphin.*)

DAN: Hiya, fella!

HELEN: About the dolphin . . .

DAN: They got an experiment book they write in.

HELEN: Where?

DAN: I don't know.

HELEN: Find it and bring it to me in the animals' morgue. Please.

DAN: I'll try. I'll try, but I got other things to do, you know.
(HELEN *slips out the door and makes it safely back into the specimen room.* DAN *rummages through the desk and finally finds the folder. He is able to sneak into the specimen room.*)

DAN: Here.
(HELEN *grabs the folder and starts going through it.* DAN *turns and is about to go back out into the hall when he sees that* MISS MORAY *has stopped reading.* HELEN *skims through more of the folder. It is a bulky affair. She stops at a page discussing uses of dolphins.* MISS MORAY *gets up from the desk and heads for the specimen-room door.*)

DAN: She's coming.

HELEN: Maybe you'd better hide. Get behind the table. Here, take the book.
(DAN *ducks down behind one of the specimen*

*tables, and* HELEN *starts scrubbing away.* MISS
MORAY *opens the door.*)

MISS MORAY: Perk-You-Up time, Helen. Tell
Dan, please. He's in the laboratory.
(HELEN *moves to the lab door, opens it, and calls
into the empty room.*)

HELEN: Perk-You-Up time.

MISS MORAY: Tell him we have ladyfingers.

HELEN: We have ladyfingers.

MISS MORAY: Such a strange thing to call a con-
fectionery, isn't it? It's almost macabre.

HELEN: Miss Moray ...

MISS MORAY: Yes, Helen?

HELEN: I was wondering why they wanna talk
with ...

MISS MORAY: Now now now!

HELEN: I mean, supposing dolphins *did* talk?

MISS MORAY: Well, like fishing, Helen. If we could communicate with dolphins, they might be willing to herd fish for us. The fishing industry would be revolutionized.

HELEN: Is that all?

MISS MORAY: All? Heavens, no. They'd be a blessing to the human race. A blessing. They would be worshipped in oceanography. Checking the Gulf Stream . . . taking water temperatures, depths, salinity readings. To say nothing of the contributions they could make in marine biology, navigation, linguistics! Oh, Helen, it gives me the chills.

HELEN: It'd be good if they talked?

MISS MORAY: God's own blessing.
(DAN *opens the lab doors and yells over* HELEN's *head to* MISS MORAY.)

DAN: I got everything except the head vise. They can't saw through the skull bone without the head vise.

MISS MORAY: Did you look on five? They had it

there last week for . . . what they did to the St. Bernard.

(*From the laboratory, music drifts out. They try to talk over it.*)

DAN: I looked on five.

MISS MORAY: You come with me. It must have been staring you in the face.

(DAN *and* MISS MORAY *get on the elevator.*)

MISS MORAY: We'll be right back, Helen.

(*The doors close and* HELEN *hurries into the laboratory. She stops just inside the door, and it is obvious that she is angry.*)

DOLPHIN: Boooooooooook.

HELEN: I looked at your book. I looked at your book all right!

DOLPHIN: Boooooooooook.

HELEN: And you want to know what I think? I don't think much of you, that's what I think.

DOLPHIN: Boooooooooook.

HELEN: Oh, shut up. Book book book book book. I'm not interested. You eat yourself silly—but to get a little fish for hungry humans is just too much for you. Well, I'm going to tell 'em you can talk.
(*The dolphin moves in the tank, lets out a few warning bubbles.*)

HELEN: You don't like that, eh? Well, I don't like lazy selfish people, mammals or animals.
(*The dolphin looks increasingly desperate and begins to make loud* blatt *and* beep *sounds. He struggles in the tank.*)

HELEN: Cut it out—you're getting water all over the floor.

DOLPHIN: Booooooooook!
(HELEN *looks at the folder on the desk. She picks it up, opens it, closes it, and sets it down again.*)

HELEN: I guess you don't like us. I guess you'd die rather than help us . . .

DOLPHIN: Hate.

HELEN: I guess you do hate us . . .
(*She returns to the folder.*)

HELEN (*reading*): Military implications . . . war . . . plant mines in enemy waters . . . deliver atomic warheads . . . war . . . nuclear torpedoes . . . attach bombs to submarines . . . terrorize enemy waters . . . war. . . . They're already thinking about ways to use you for war. Is that why you can't talk to them? (*pause*) What did you talk to me for? (*pause*) You won't talk to them, but you . . . you talk to me because . . . you want something . . . there's something . . . I can do?

DOLPHIN: Hamm . . .

HELEN: What?

DOLPHIN: Hamm . . .

HELEN: Ham? I thought you ate fish.

DOLPHIN (*moving with annoyance*): Ham . . . purrrr.

HELEN: Ham . . . purrrr? I don't know what you're talking about.

DOLPHIN (*even more annoyed*): Ham . . . purrrr.

HELEN: Ham . . . purrrr. What's a purrrr?
(*Confused and scared, she returns to scrubbing the hall floor just as the doors of the elevator open, revealing* MISS MORAY, DAN, *and* MR. FRIDGE. DAN *pushes a dissection table loaded with shiny instruments toward the lab.*)

MISS MORAY: Is the good doctor in yet?

MR. FRIDGE: He's getting the nicotine mustard on nine. I'll see if he needs assistance.

MISS MORAY: I'll come with you. You'd better leave now, Helen. It's time. (*She smiles and the elevator doors close.*)

DAN (*pushing the dissection table through the lab doors*): I never left a dirty head vise. She's trying to say I left it like that.

HELEN: Would you listen a minute? Ham . . . purrrr. Do you know what a ham . . . purrrr is?

DAN: The only hamper I ever heard of is out in the hall.
(HELEN *darts to the door, opens it, and sees the hamper at the end of the hall.*)

HELEN: The hamper!

DAN: Kazinski left the high-altitude chamber dirty once, and I got blamed for that, too. (*He exits.*)

HELEN (*rushing to the dolphin*): You want me to do something with the hamper. What? To get it? To put . . . you want me to put you in it? But what'll I do with you? Where can I take you?

DOLPHIN: Sea . . .

HELEN: See? See what?

DOLPHIN: Sea . . .

HELEN: I don't know what you're talking about. They'll be back in a minute. I don't know what to do!

DOLPHIN: Sea . . . sea . . .

HELEN: See? . . . The sea! That's what you're talking about! The river . . . to the sea!
(*She darts into the hall and heads for the hamper. Quickly she pushes it into the lab, and just as she gets through the doors unseen,* MISS MORAY *gets off the elevator.*)

ABADABA

MISS MORAY: Helen?
(*She starts down the hall. Enters the lab. The curtain is closed in front of the tank.*)

MISS MORAY: Helen? Are you here? Helen?
(*She sees nothing and is about to leave when she hears a movement behind the curtain. She looks down and sees HELEN's shoes. MISS MORAY moves to the curtain and pulls it open. There is HELEN with her arms around the front part of the dolphin, lifting it a good part of the way out of the water.*)

MISS MORAY: Helen, what do you think you're hugging?
(HELEN *drops the dolphin back into the tank.*)

MR. FRIDGE (*entering*): Is anything wrong, Miss Moray?

MISS MORAY: No . . . nothing wrong. Nothing at all. Just a little spilled water.
(HELEN and MISS MORAY *grab sponges from the lab sink and begin to wipe up the water around the tank.* DR. CROCUS *enters and begins to fill a hypodermic syringe while* MR. FRIDGE *expertly gets all equipment into place.* DAN *enters.*)

MR. FRIDGE: Would you like to get an encephalogram during the death process, Dr. Crocus?

DR. CROCUS: Why not?
(MR. FRIDGE *begins to implant electrodes in the dolphin's head. The dolphin commences making high-pitched distress signals.*)

MISS MORAY: Come, Helen. I'll see you to the elevator.
(MISS MORAY *leads her out to the hall.* HELEN *gets on her coat and kerchief.*)

MISS MORAY: Frankly, Helen, I'm deeply disappointed. I'd hoped that by being lenient with you—and heaven knows I have been—you'd develop a heightened loyalty to our team.

HELEN (*bursting into tears and going to the elevator*): Leave me alone.

MISS MORAY (*softening as she catches up to her*): You really are a nice person, Helen. A very nice person. But to be simple and nice in a world where great minds are giant-stepping the micro- and macrocosms, well—one would expect you'd have the humility to yield in unquestioning awe. I truly am very fond of you, Helen, but you're fired. Call Personnel after nine A.M.

(*As* MISS MORAY *disappears into the laboratory, the record starts to play.*)

RECORD: "Let me call you sweetheart,
I'm in love with you.
Let me hear you whisper . . ."
(*The record is roughly interrupted. Instead of getting on the elevator,* HELEN *whirls around and barges into the lab.*)

HELEN: Who do you think you are? (*pause*) Who do you think you *are*? (*pause*) I think you're a pack of killers, that's what I think.

MISS MORAY: Doctor, I assure you this is the first psychotic outbreak she's made. She did the entire brass strip . . .

HELEN: I'm very tired of being a nice person, Miss Moray. I'm going to report you to the ASPCA, or somebody, because . . . I've decided I don't like you cutting the heads off mice and sawing through skulls of St. Bernards . . . and if being a nice person is just not saying anything and letting you pack of butchers run around doing whatever you want, then I don't want to be nice anymore. (*pause*) You gotta be very stupid people to need an animal to talk before you know just from looking at it that it's saying something . . . that it knows what pain feels like. I'd like to see you all with a few electrodes in your heads. Being nice isn't any good. (*looking at dolphin*) They just kill you off if you do that. And that's being a coward. You gotta talk back. You gotta speak up against what's wrong and bad, or you can't ever stop it. At least you've gotta try. (*She bursts into tears.*)

MISS MORAY: Nothing like this has ever happened with a member of the Custodial Engineering . . . Helen, dear . . .

HELEN: Get your hands off me. (*yelling at the dolphin*) You're a coward, that's what you are. I'm going.

DOLPHIN: Looooooooooveeeeeeeee.
(*Everyone turns to stare at the dolphin.*)

DOLPHIN: Love.

DR. CROCUS: Get the recorder going.
(HELEN *pats the dolphin, exits. The laboratory becomes a bustle of activity.*)

41

DOLPHIN: Love . . .

DR. CROCUS: Is the tape going?

MR. FRIDGE: Yes, Doctor.

DOLPHIN: Love . . .

DR. CROCUS: I think that woman's got something to do with this. Get her back in here.

MISS MORAY: Oh, I fired her. She was hugging the mammal . . . and . . .

DOLPHIN: Love . . .

DR. CROCUS: Just get her. (*to* MR. FRIDGE) You're sure the machine's recording?

MISS MORAY: Doctor, I'm afraid you don't understand. That woman was hugging the mammal . . .

DR. CROCUS: Try to get another word out of it. One more word . . .

MISS MORAY: The last thing in the world I want is for our problem in Custodial Engineering to . . .

DR. CROCUS (*furious*): Will you shut up and get that washwoman back in here?

MISS MORAY: Immediately, Doctor.
(*She hurries out of the lab.* HELEN *is at the end of the hall waiting for the elevator.*)

MISS MORAY: Helen? Oh, Helen? Don't you want to hear what the dolphin has to say? He's so cute! Dr. Crocus thinks that his talking might have something to do with you. Wouldn't that be exciting? (*pause*) Please, Helen. The doctor . . .

HELEN: Don't talk to me, do you mind?

MISS MORAY: It was only in the heat of argument that I . . . of course, you won't be discharged. All right? Please, Helen, you'll embarrass me . . .
(*The elevator doors open and* HELEN *gets on to face* MISS MORAY. *She looks at her a moment and then lifts her hand to press the button for the ground floor.*)

MISS MORAY: Don't you dare . . . Helen, the team needs you, don't you see? You've done so well—the brass strip, the floors. The floors have never looked so good. Ever. Helen, please. What will I do if you leave?

HELEN: Why don't you get a rug?

(HELEN *helps slam the elevator doors in* MISS MORAY'S *face as the lights go down, ending the play*.)

812
Zin        Zindel, Paul
           Let me hear you whisper:
           a play

9413